Swop!

by

Hilary McKay

Illustrated by Kirstin Holbrow

You do not need to read this page – just get on with the book!

First published in 2006 in Great Britain by
Barrington Stoke Ltd
www.barringtonstoke.co.uk

This edition based on *Swop!* published by
Barrington Stoke in 2005

ISBN 1-842994-09-3
13 digit ISBN 978-1-84299-409-2

Printed in Great Britain by Bell & Bain Ltd

MEET THE AUTHOR – HILARY McKAY

What is your favourite animal?
Fox
What is your favourite boy's name?
Jim
What is your favourite girl's name?
Bella
What is your favourite food?
Apples
What is your favourite music?
Classic rock and Bach
What is your favourite hobby?
Natural history

MEET THE ILLUSTRATOR – KIRSTIN HOLBROW

What is your favourite animal?
My dog, Pewter Plum
What is your favourite boy's name?
George
What is your favourite girl's name?
Beryl
What is your favourite food?
Shellfish
What is your favourite music?
Ambient techno
What is your favourite hobby?
Rowing on the river Wye

For Emily and Bella

Contents

Chapter 1
Emily and Tom

Emily lived with her Gran and her twin brother Tom and a wicked old lady called Aunty Bess. They had a little house just out of the town. A road went past their garden gate and on down to the sea.

Emily and Tom had never seen the sea. And they had never seen the town. The only place they ever went was to school. Wicked old Aunty Bess would not let them.

Wicked old Aunty Bess was the boss in the little house.

Emily and Tom's Gran never said anything. All day long she sat in a rocking chair by the door of the little house. She gazed for hours at the three apple trees that grew in the garden. When it was sunny she sat in the sun. When it was raining she sat under a big umbrella.

Emily and Tom had no toys or books or pets.

"Toys and books and pets are for good children!" said wicked old Aunty Bess. "Birthdays and Christmas and having friends round to play are what good children get! So squish squash! None for you!"

She was not fair. Emily looked at her. She was thinking, *Squish squash to you!*

Tom looked at Aunty Bess, *How bad are we?* he was thinking.

Not that bad, thought Tom.

What was good in Tom and Emily's life was the road that went past their garden gate. A lot of interesting men, women and children went along that road. They were going to the sea from the town, or to the town from the sea. Every day Emily and Tom saw them go past.

Chapter 2
The Gypsy

One day Emily and Tom saw a lovely gypsy-man go past. He had gold ear-rings and a red shirt and black eyes. He wore tall boots with heels that clacked, and he strode along with his hands in his pockets. He whistled a tune as he went.

Emily heard the gypsy coming from far away. She ran to the gate and there he was. He was leading a small grey donkey.

What Emily liked best was swopping.

Emily was a wild and fun swopper.

The gypsy seemed to know this without being told. He looked over the fence at Emily, and he said, "It's a lovely sunny day! Just the day for a swop!"

"Yes," said Emily, nodding her head.

"Yes," said the gypsy, and he whistled a bit more of his tune. Then he said, "So? Would you like a donkey?"

Emily nodded even harder.

The gypsy looked around the garden. There was nothing in it but the apple trees, and Tom, and silent little Gran in her rocking chair.

"You could never carry the apple trees away," said Emily. "And I'm not letting Tom go!"

"What about the old lady?" asked the gypsy. "She looks a nice, quiet old lady. I could just do with one like that."

He looked at Emily and gave her a wink. Emily winked back and nodded again.

Then all in a flash the donkey was in the garden, and Emily and Tom's Gran was being jumped over the gate by the gypsy. And then both of them were gone.

That was Emily's best swop ever. She was only six years old and she did it all by herself.

"Emily!" yelled wicked old Aunty Bess, when she found out what Emily had done.

"Are you telling me you swopped your Gran for a donkey?"

"Yes, Aunty Bess," said Emily. "That's what I did. Didn't I, Tom?"

"Yes, Aunty Bess," said Tom.

"Tom!" yelled wicked old Aunty Bess. She was even more cross. "Are you telling me you JUST LET EMILY DO IT?"

"Yes, Aunty Bess," said Tom. "We thought it was a good swop. We hoped you would be glad."

Aunty Bess was not glad at all. She said the donkey would have to go. But the donkey stayed. It lived in the garden under the apple trees and Emily and Tom loved it more than all the toys and books and pets in the world.

"Don't ever let me catch you chatting with a gypsy man again!" said Aunty Bess, when she gave Emily and Tom their supper of dry bread and water. "But I'm not sure this man was a gypsy! He sounds more like a PIRATE to me!"

"We won't do it again, Aunty Bess," Emily and Tom told her. But every day they kept looking down the road. They hoped another gypsy would come whistling by.

Chapter 3

The Spanish Lady and the Man with the Owls

Emily and Tom did not see the gypsy-man again for a long, long time.

They stayed in the little house, with nothing much going on, until they were ten years old. By then the donkey was very fat, and they were very thin. Wicked old Aunty Bess had stopped giving them bread with their water for supper, and she had stopped

giving them water with their bread for breakfast. But they did have a secret store of apples from the apple trees in the garden, and on school days they had school dinners.

By the time Emily was ten her swopping was wilder than ever.

A Spanish lady with red and orange skirts and high-heeled shoes came tapping along the road. Ever since the gypsy-man went away Emily had been teaching herself to whistle his tune. She could do it very well by now. Emily swopped the tune with the Spanish lady and got a violin. She wanted the violin for Tom. He loved tunes as much as she did, but he could never learn how to whistle.

Very soon after Tom got his violin, a tall thin man with two owls came by. He swopped a violin book for a bag of apples.

It was a very good book to learn from. Tom soon learnt to play his violin. But the music made wicked old Aunty Bess very cross. She didn't believe Emily and Tom when they told her about the Spanish lady and the tall thin man with the two owls. She spat and said, "Arr! Squish squash! I never heard such lies! They sound just like PIRATES to me!"

Emily had begun to think a lot about pirates.

Wicked old Aunty Bess did not let Tom play his violin in the house. He had to play in the garden and the noise made every dog that lived between the town and the sea sit down and howl. Emily and Tom loved it when the dogs howled. They had still never seen the sea, or gone into the town. When they asked if they could do these things wicked old Aunty Bess said, "Just you try and I'll cook you and eat you! And then I'll use your bones to light the fire."

Emily and Tom did not think she would use their bones to light the fire. They did not think she could light the fire. She always made them do it. But they did believe she would eat them. Wicked old Aunty Bess ate anything. They had once seen her eat a dead cat that she found. So they did not try to run away.

Chapter 4
The Sailor

It was hard for Emily and Tom never to have presents on their birthday. It was very bad when they were ten. At school everyone knew it was a very exciting age to be.

The other children had lots of presents and extra good parties when they were ten. They did not ask Emily and Tom to come to the parties because everyone knew they never went out. Anyway, Emily and Tom had nothing to wear for parties. They always wore old rags to school.

"I don't care," said Emily, but Tom knew she did care. For their tenth birthday he made her a lovely necklace out of silver grass and some pretty beads he found in the mud at the back of the house. Tom was a kind boy. He was very good at making things.

Emily was not good at making things. This did not matter a bit because she was so fantastic at swopping.

For Tom's tenth birthday she swopped her own long gold hair for a tiny spotty kitten. He had a soft round face and tufty red fur.

Emily did not like her long hair. One day she cut it all off and hung it over the fence just as a sailor came rolling down the road.

The sailor had blue tattoos all over his arms. When he saw Emily's long hair hanging on the fence he told Emily it was just what he needed to fix the rigging on his ship.

"What's rigging?" asked Emily, and the kind sailor told her all about ropes and sails and flags and knots. Wicked old Aunty Bess came home and found him still talking to Emily. Aunty Bess was very rude to him. She said to Emily, "What did I tell you about chatting with gypsies?"

The sailor was very polite. He said, "I'm not a gypsy, madam. I'm a sailor from over the seven seas."

"Squish squash, as if I cared!" snapped Aunty Bess. "You look more like a PIRATE to me!"

"Thank you, madam," said the sailor, and he looked very happy. Emily knew then that a pirate was a fantastic thing to be.

Chapter 5
The Silver Woman

Tom was very happy with his little spotty kitten. Wicked old Aunty Bess was not. She said, "I shall drown it in a bucket of water."

But she had no luck with that plan. When the kitten was awake it moved as fast as magic, and when it went to sleep it lay on the little donkey's back. The donkey kicked wicked old Aunty Bess if she came anywhere near. The little spotty kitten grew and grew. They called it Spotty.

"How lucky that Spotty loves bread and water and apple cores," said Tom. "He's very big and strong. I think he's bigger than other cats.

"Yes, he is," said Emily. Then they both stroked Spotty. He purred and stood on his back paws and licked their faces.

"His spots are like roses!" said Tom. "I think he is a rare sort of cat. I shall look him up in a book at school."

"Stop fussing over that horrid cat and come and cut my toe-nails!" yelled wicked old Aunty Bess out of the window. "And then you can rub my back and cook my supper! And bring me another bottle of beer! I feel like being looked after tonight!"

Looking after wicked old Aunty Bess was very hard work. By the time she had got drunk and gone to bed, Emily and Tom were worn out.

Tom sat on the steps and played long slow notes on his violin. Spotty climbed onto the top of the roof. He lay with two paws hanging down on each side and his tail around the chimney. All the dogs for miles around began to howl. Emily went and stood by the gate and whistled the gypsy's tune.

Down the road came a thin silver woman. She moved with a sound like the wind. As she came closer Emily saw that she was a little bit see-through, like cloudy glass.

"Are you a ghost?" asked Emily, trying to be brave.

"Oh, no," said the silver woman. "I just came because I heard the music."

Then she looked hard at Emily's necklace of silver grass and pretty beads, and asked, "What would you swop that for?"

All at once, Spotty suddenly stood up on the roof. He looked huge. The donkey stamped his hooves. All the dogs stopped howling.

Emily held her necklace tight with both hands. "I won't swop this," she said. "Not for anything in the world."

"Good girl," said the silver woman. "That was what I hoped you'd say."

Spotty lay down again and the donkey stood still and all the dogs began to howl once more. From under her cloak, the silver woman took out a bunch of carrots, some

bread and a pot of honey. Then she swopped them all for a drink of water.

So that night Emily and Tom and Spotty and the donkey had supper under the apple trees.

Wicked old Aunty Bess was fast asleep. She never knew anything about it.

"What a lovely silver woman," said Tom, full of bread and honey for the first time in his life.

"Yes," nodded Emily, and smiled. "But I expect Aunty Bess would tell us she was a pirate."

Chapter 6
Spotty

There was no peace for Emily and Tom at the little house after the silver woman came. Tom did not forget his plan to find out more about Spotty in a book at school. He started the very next day. First he looked in a book called *Pet Cats and How to Care for Them.*

There were no cats like Spotty in that book.

Then he looked in a book called *Pet Cats and Cats in the Wild.*

There were no cats like Spotty in that book either.

Then he found another book. *Big Cats.*

"Don't look in that book!" begged Emily. "What does it matter what Spotty is? Let's just love him like we always have!"

"OK," said Tom. He could see she was upset so he shut the book.

That night they went home to love Spotty just like they always had. Spotty was asleep in the middle of the roof of the little house. And the roof was sagging. When Spotty saw Emily and Tom he yowled because he was so glad to see them. And then he stood up and stretched. He stretched his front paws forward and he could just touch one end of the roof. Then he stretched his back paws backwards, and he could just touch the other end of the roof.

Then Spotty jumped about on the top of the house and the roof sagged even more.

Emily and Tom always slept in the attic on piles of grass they picked in the garden.

That night when they lay down on their little grass beds, they saw that the roof was sagging so low in the middle that it almost touched their noses.

"I *must* find out more about Spotty!" said Tom.

"Yes, I think you must," said Emily.

The picture in *Big Cats* that looked most like Spotty was of a leopard. The leopard had rose shaped spots, just like Spotty. It had huge paws and huge claws, just like Spotty. The book called *Big Cats* said that of all the big cats, leopards were the most dangerous and wild.

"Oh, Emily!" said Tom. "Aunty Bess will never let Spotty stay if he's a leopard!"

"Don't let's tell her," said Emily.

"But Spotty might eat her!"

"What if he does?" said Emily.

Tom did not like Aunty Bess, but he did not want Spotty to eat her. He did not think Spotty should eat anyone and he told Emily so.

"Spotty might not be a leopard at all," said Emily. "He isn't quite like the leopard in the book."

Tom looked at the picture again and said, "His paws are!"

"The one in the book," said Emily, "doesn't have wings."

Tom looked at Emily. Then he looked at Spotty. Then he looked at Emily again. She was right. The tufts on Spotty's back had grown into wings. And the next day he looked up Spotty in a book called *Most Dangerous Magic Beasts*.

"He's a rare sort of griffin," he told Emily in bed that night. But wicked old Aunty Bess was spying on them. She heard what Tom said.

"A griffin!" she yelled. She was mad with anger. "A griffin! Only a PIRATE would give a child a griffin for a pet!"

"Do you think she's right?" said Tom.

"I hope so," said Emily.

Chapter 7
Gran

The next morning wicked old Aunty Bess said she knew she should have drowned Spotty when they first got him.

When Spotty heard that, he spat and showed his teeth and claws.

"He's not safe," said wicked old Aunty Bess.

"Don't worry," said Tom. "We won't let him hurt you."

"What will I do when you're at school?" asked Aunty Bess. "What will he do then? Well, you will just have to stay at home!"

Emily and Tom went white. No school would mean no school dinners. They would only have bread and water and apples to eat.

"Children have to go to school, Aunty Bess," said Emily. "It's the law."

"We'll see about that!" said Aunty Bess, and she wrote a note which said,

Dear School,

Emily and Tom will not be coming to
school any more.

They have to stay home to make
sure their pet griffin
does not eat me.

Yours truly,
A. Bess

P.S. No more school dinners for
Emily and Tom.

School sent a note back saying,

That's cool.

Love School.

P.S. No more school dinners for Emily and Tom.

"So ha, ha! Squish squash!" said Aunty Bess. She waved the letter over her head. "Told you so!"

Emily wanted to run away.

Tom did not. Sometimes he thought Emily was too brave. But he did not say that, because he liked her the way she was.

Perhaps he should be more brave. He said, "Aunty Bess said she would eat us if we tried to run away."

So they stayed, and they were very hungry. And as they got more and more hungry, Spotty grew more and more wild. He got so wild that he scared the donkey, even though they had always been friends.

One night the donkey was so jumpy and jittery he did a very foolish thing.

He ate all the bark off the apple trees.

The apple trees died.

"We *must* run away," said Emily. "There will only be bread and water to eat now. Don't be scared of Aunty Bess. I am sure she won't eat us. Spotty won't let her."

"No," said Tom. "I don't think he would. But poor Aunty Bess! She would be so lonely without us!"

Sometimes Emily thought Tom was too kind. But she did not say that, because she liked him the way he was.

So they stayed. And they were very, very hungry. And they were quite unhappy, too.

Then, just when things were really bad, Emily and Tom heard someone singing along the road. Screechy sort of singing. And they ran to the gate just in time to see a little old lady jump right over it. Gran.

Gran had come back, and she was not at all the same Gran. They didn't know where she had been, but she must have had a very good time there. She smoked a big pipe, and she sang rude songs. She danced clattering dances on the kitchen floor. She had a big rope which she used as a lasso.

"She's bonkers!" said Emily

When wicked old Aunty Bess and Gran saw each other they started to shout at each other. Gran tried to lasso Aunty Bess with the rope.

"Ha, ha! Missed again!" shouted wicked old Aunty Bess. "Squish squash! I'm the boss in this house!"

Then Gran and wicked old Aunty Bess chased each other round and round the dead apple trees, and all over the house, and onto the sagging roof and off again.

They looked as if they were having fun. But the noise was awful.

Tom couldn't hear his violin when he played it. The dogs that lived between the town and the sea couldn't hear themselves howl. And Spotty spat and hissed on the roof, while the donkey brayed in the garden.

"Tom," said Emily, "we must run away *now*! Gran will stop Aunty Bess from being lonely. And Spotty will stop her eating us."

So they did.

They ran away.

They jumped over the gate and ran down the road that led to the sea. Tom took his violin, and Emily carried his violin book, and Spotty and the donkey ran after them.

Chapter 8
The Pirate

Emily and Tom ran and ran. They ran away from wicked Aunty Bess and Gran and the little house by the road. And at last they saw the sea, the huge, shining, silver sea. They gazed and gazed and gazed. At last Tom said, "We should have run away ages ago."

But Emily shook her head, "No. It would have been unkind."

And then they walked slowly down to the edge of the sea.

A ship was waiting there. A sailing ship, green and gold with two tall masts. It rocked on the tide. The sails were red and white striped. The flags that blew above the sails were black as night. At the front of the ship was a golden griffin made of wood. On the decks were bins full of apples and stacks of hay. A long plank went from the ship to the shore, and at the end of the plank stood a PIRATE!

They knew he was a pirate because he had a black hat with a white feather. He had gold teeth that sparkled in his smile, and sea-blue eyes, and a spy-glass and a cutlass. He had a parrot on his arm.

When the pirate saw Emily and Tom, he took off his hat and tossed it high in the air. "HERE YOU ARE AT LAST!" he shouted.

Then lots of people came up onto the deck. The gypsy and the sailor, the Spanish lady and the man with the owls. Last of all came the silver woman. They rushed Emily and Tom up the plank and onto the ship. There were lots of things they wanted to ask.

"Was the donkey any good?" asked the gypsy.

"Oh yes," said Emily. "Thank you very much. He saved Spotty from being drowned in a bucket!"

"And what about the violin?" said the Spanish lady.

"It was just what I needed," said Tom. "Because I've tried and tried but I just can't whistle."

"And the book?" asked the man with the owls.

"I couldn't have learnt to play the violin without the book," said Tom.

"And what about Spotty?" asked the sailor.

"Spotty has been fantastic!" said Emily. "I think he saved us from being eaten! And look how big he's grown!"

"And did you like the bread and honey?" asked the silver woman.

"Very, very, very much," said Emily and Tom.

"I'm sorry about Gran," the gypsy told them. "I had to let her go. She just made too much noise!"

"I think she'll be just right for Aunty Bess," said Tom.

"Now," said the pirate, giving the parrot to Emily and the spy-glass to Tom, "we're about to set sail! Will you come along with us? What do you think? Will you swop a life on shore for a life on the seven seas?"

He put his hands on his hips and looked down at Emily and Tom.

"Yes, yes!" shouted Tom at once.

"And what about you?" the pirate asked Emily, and he winked. Emily had known for a long, long time that it would be fantastic to be a pirate. So she winked back at the pirate and nodded and smiled.

That is the end. They sailed away with the pirate, and Spotty and the donkey and

all the friends who had looked after them so well, and they lived happily ever after.

And Gran lived happily ever after too.

And so did wicked old Aunty Bess.

They mended the roof and grew some more apple trees and took turns with the lasso and the rocking chair.

Sometimes, when a storm was blowing, Emily and Tom would hear their voices, carried on the wind from far away.

"Ha ha! Squish squash! Missed again!"

And awful screechy singing.

And all the dogs howling between the town and the sea.

If you loved this story, why don't you read ...

The Smallest Horse in the World

by Jeremy Strong

Bella loves her picture of a horse. But when it breaks, a real, tiny horse jumps out! Can Bella keep her new friend a secret – and help her find a home?

4u2read.ok!

You can order this book directly from our website
www.barringtonstoke.co.uk